nickelodeon™

PAW Patrol™

5-Minute Stories Collection

Random House 🏠 New York

CONTENTS

Marshall to the Rescue!

Illustrated by MJ Illustrations

It was an exciting day at the Lookout. A flock of geese was stopping overnight to rest.

Rocky built a big nest for the birds to sleep in.

Rubble used his shovel to fill the nest with bread for them to eat.

Marshall was so excited, he accidentally tumbled into the nest. "The geese are coming!" he shouted.

The geese flew in and landed, honking happily. *Honk! Honk!*
They started pecking at the pieces of bread right away. One
tired goose settled down into the nest to relax.

"She likes your nest, Rocky," Ryder said, patting the pup
on the head. Rocky smiled, proud of his good work.

But a baby goose wandered away from the rest of the flock.
He waddled into a blue bucket—and rolled down a hill!

"I'll get him!" Marshall announced, racing after the bucket.
But as he ran, his feet got tangled up. Marshall *and* the little
gosling ended up bouncing down the hill!

When they reached the bottom, they were both a little dizzy.
The gosling's eyes rolled around.

"Are you okay, fuzzy little guy?" Marshall asked.

Cheep! Cheep! the goose replied with a nod.

"Hey!" Marshall exclaimed. "Fuzzy is a great name for you!"
He nudged the gosling with his nose. "Back to your family, Fuzzy!"

Marshall took Fuzzy back up the hill to the Lookout.
"Nice work, Marshall!" Ryder said.
Marshall introduced the little goose to the rest of the PAW Patrol.
Fuzzy liked all the pups, but Marshall was definitely his favorite.
Skye chuckled. "Marshall, it looks like you have a new BGFF—
Best Goose Friend Forever!" All the pups laughed.

For the rest of the day, the two friends did everything together. The little goose followed Marshall everywhere he went.

When Marshall washed his fire truck, Fuzzy polished the window with his tail feathers . . .

. . . until Marshall accidentally "washed" the little goose with his hose.

"Oops!" Marshall said. "Sorry, Fuzzy!"

That evening, Marshall walked back to the nest with Fuzzy on his head.

"Okay, Fuzzy," he said, bending so Fuzzy could hop off. "Time to hit the hay—or, nest!"

Fuzzy jumped up and down on Marshall's head. *Cheep! Cheep!* He didn't want his new friend to leave!

"I suppose I could sleep out here," Marshall said. "But just this once." He curled up, and soon they were both asleep.

First thing the next morning, while Marshall was still asleep, Fuzzy wandered off, looking for food. He was hungry!

When Marshall woke up, he looked around for his friend. No Fuzzy! He called his name, but the goose didn't answer.

Marshall ran to Ryder. "Fuzzy is gone!" he said. "We have to find him before his flock leaves!"

Ryder called the PAW Patrol to the Lookout.

"Our goose friends have to fly south for the winter," he explained. "But they're missing one little goose. If we don't find Fuzzy fast, they'll have to leave without him! Chase, I need you to call Fuzzy with your megaphone. Marshall, Fuzzy would follow you anywhere. I need you to help look for him, too!"

Outside the Lookout, Chase broadcast a goose honk
through his megaphone, but Fuzzy didn't answer.

Marshall sniffed the ground, searching for clues. He
found one of Fuzzy's feathers! Ryder picked it up, and
Chase took a whiff.

AH-CHOO! Chase sneezed. "Sorry—I'm a little
allergic to feathers." He took a few more sniffs, sneezed,
and announced, "He went this way!"

Marshall, Chase, and Ryder jumped into their vehicles and raced across Adventure Bay. Their sirens blared as they followed Fuzzy's feather trail. This was an emergency!

Suddenly, Marshall heard chirping. Fuzzy was on the roof of the train station! He had a piece of bread in his beak, and two seagulls were trying to steal it.

"Fuzzy, fly down here!" Marshall called.

"He can't!" Ryder said. "A plastic soda-can ring is wrapped around his wing! Marshall, use your ladder to help get Fuzzy down!"

Marshall extended the ladder on his fire truck, which scared away the seagulls. He climbed up the ladder. But Fuzzy slipped on the edge of the roof and fell off!

"Use your helmet!" Ryder cried.

Marshall caught Fuzzy in his fire helmet.

"Sweet catch, Marshall!" Ryder cheered.

"Now let's get this off you," Ryder said, carefully pulling the plastic ring from Fuzzy. He was free again!

The gosling flapped his wings, flew into the air, and landed on Marshall's head. Marshall laughed.

The PAW Patrol raced back to the Lookout. They had to get there before Fuzzy's flock flew away!

But they were too late—the geese had just left! Fuzzy would have to flap fast to catch up to them.

Fuzzy didn't want to go, and Marshall didn't want him to leave, either.

"A little gosling belongs with his family," Ryder said.

Marshall agreed, and Ryder quickly came up with a plan to return Fuzzy to his flock.

"Let's take to the sky!" Skye exclaimed as her helicopter rose into the air, lifting Marshall in a harness.

Cheep! Cheep! Fuzzy flapped his wings and followed Marshall through the sky. Soon they caught up with the flock of geese.

"Goodbye, Fuzzy!" Marshall called as Fuzzy joined the flock. "Have a safe flight, you silly goose!"

Back at the Lookout, the pups played jump rope.

"You guys did an awesome job today," Ryder said. "What a bunch of good pups!"

Marshall missed Fuzzy, but he knew his little friend would visit whenever his family flew overhead. Until then, Marshall had his *paw*-some pup pals to keep him company!

High-Flying Skye

Illustrated by MJ Illustrations

Skye was flying high over the Lookout. She was really excited because her hero, stunt pilot Ace Sorensen, was coming to the air show in Adventure Bay.

"Trick flying is the best!" she exclaimed.

Down on the ground, Marshall wasn't sure he agreed. "The only things I like to fly are kites!" he said.

Ryder got a call on his PupPad. It was Ace Sorensen, the stunt pilot! Her plane was having engine trouble, and she needed the PAW Patrol's help in finding a place to land.

"We're on it!" Ryder declared. "No job is too big, no pup is too small!"

Ryder called the pups to the Lookout and told them about Ace. He needed Skye's helicopter and night-vision goggles.

"This pup's got to fly!" Skye shouted, eager to help her hero.

Ryder also needed Chase to make a runway with his spotlight and traffic cones.

"Chase is on the case!" he barked.

Finally, Ryder asked Rocky to help fix Ace's plane.

"Green means go!" Rocky cheered.

The sun was setting as Skye zoomed through the clouds in her helicopter. She scanned the sky with her night-vision goggles and spotted Ace's airplane. "There she is now!"

Black smoke poured out of the plane's engine, making it hard for Ace to see. Skye flew in front of her. "Follow me!" she called, leading the way to Farmer Yumi's Farm.

At the farm, Ryder, Chase, and Rocky prepared a runway for Ace to land on. Chase set up his orange safety cones to mark off the landing strip.

"Great job, Chase!" Ryder said. "But Ace will need to see this runway in the dark!"

"Rocky, do you have any old flashlights in your truck?"
Ryder asked.

"I've got a bunch!" Rocky said. He taped the flashlights
to the cones with Ryder's help.

Ryder called Skye on his PupPad. "Watch for the runway
lights!"

"Roger that!" Skye answered.

Skye zoomed through the night and spotted the glowing landing strip. But when she and Ace started to fly down toward it, they heard a loud BOOM!

Ace's plane shook! Sparks sizzled along the wing!

"I'll have to parachute out!" Ace radioed to the team.

But Ryder thought parachuting in the dark was too dangerous. "Ace, have you ever done the wing-walking stunt?" he asked.

"Ace is the greatest wing-walker in the whole world," Skye reported.

"Awesome!" Ryder exclaimed. He told Skye to lower her towline and safety harness.

Ace climbed onto the wing. Skye lowered her safety
harness, but Ace couldn't reach it!

"I'm going to jump with my parachute!" Ace called.

"No! We can do this!" Skye insisted.

She flew as close to Ace as she could, and the stunt pilot
grabbed the harness!

As Skye flew her to the farm, Ace called Ryder. "Could you check on *Amelia*?"

"Sure," Ryder said. "But who's *Amelia*?"

"My plane!" Ace answered.

Ryder tracked the plane on his PupPad and saw that it was heading for the bay! "Let's get *Amelia* before she sinks!"

Skye gently set Ace down at the farm. "Thanks, Skye!" Ace called.

"No problem, Ace!" the pilot pup called back. To herself, she whispered, "I can't believe I saved my hero!"

At the bay, *Amelia* landed in the water. *SPLASH!*
Ryder rode out to the plane and hooked a cable to it.
"Chase, let's get *Amelia* to the beach before she sinks!"
"I'm on it!" Chase called. He turned on his winch
and pulled the plane to shore.

"*Amelia*'s in pretty rough shape," Ace said when she saw her plane. "I don't think she'll be ready for the air show tomorrow. That would take a whole team of mechanics!"

"Teammates reporting for duty!" Rocky said.

The PAW Patrol used all their tools to fix
Amelia in no time!

"Wow!" Ace said. "She's as good as the first
day we flew together! Thanks, team!"

The pups barked and howled!

"Whenever you need a paw, just yelp for help!"
Ryder said, laughing.

"I can't wait for the air show tomorrow!" Skye said.
Ace hopped onto one of the wings. "How would you like
to see my wing-walk-and-roll trick up close and personal?"
Skye thought that sounded great!

The next day was sunny and warm. The PAW Patrol watched the air show from the beach.

Except Skye! She got to watch from the backseat of Ace's plane! While she worked the controls, Ace did her amazing wing-walk-and-roll trick.

"Way to go, Ace!" Ryder shouted.

"Wow!" Rocky gasped, watching Skye zoom through the clouds. "She's so good!"

"You're all good pups," Ryder said.

The pups cheered and barked for each other as Skye and Ace zipped overhead.

GOLD RUSH PUPS!

Illustrated by MJ Illustrations

One sunny day, Rubble was digging for gold with Mayor Goodway and her Uncle Otis.

Uncle Otis's old shovel broke, and the bottom fell out of the pan he used to strain for gold.

Rubble and Mayor Goodway knew just who to call for help—the PAW Patrol!

Ryder, Chase, and Rocky zoomed to the rescue.
"We've brought the perfect tools!" Rocky said.
There was a shovel for Uncle Otis and some
old strainers everyone could use to pan for gold.
They all went to work beside the river.

Pecking at the ground, Chickaletta found a shiny nugget.
"Look!" Ryder cried. "Gold!"
They started digging near the spot where the chicken had
found the nugget. Soon Ryder and Chase had struck gold, too!
In no time at all, they had a big pile of glittering gold.

Since Chickaletta had found the first gold nugget, Mayor Goodway decided to make a big golden statue of her feathery friend.

"Good idea!" Ryder exclaimed. "C'mon, pups—the more gold we find, the bigger the statue of Chickaletta!"

In a nearby tree, Mayor Humdinger from Foggy
Bottom was spying on the pups and their friends.

"That gold is mine, because . . . um . . . I want it!"
he growled.

Mayor Humdinger planned to make a golden
statue of himself. He radioed his Kit-tastrophe
Crew. "Kittens, it's catastrophe time!"

Mayor Humdinger joined Ryder and the pup prospectors. The mean mayor snuck something into his strainer while the others searched for gold.

"What's this?" he said, pretending to be surprised. "A diamond!"

Everyone was amazed by the mayor's discovery.

While Ryder, Mayor Goodway, Chickaletta, and the pups studied the diamond, Mayor Humdinger's kittens went to work.

Behind the others' backs, the Kit-tastrophe Crew loaded all the gold nuggets onto a cart.

"Let me take a look at that diamond," Uncle Otis asked. Mayor Goodway handed the sparkling jewel to him. He peered at it closely. "This is no diamond," he announced. "It's just rock candy!"

The friends turned around just in time to see Mayor Humdinger driving off with all the gold!

Ryder and the pups jumped on their vehicles to chase Mayor Humdinger. The PAW Patrol was on the roll!

But the thief was already out of sight. "Chase, we need your drone!" Ryder exclaimed.

Chase hit a button, launching his drone into the air. It flew high enough to track Mayor Humdinger and his kittens.

The gold-snatchers raced up the mountain to their secret hideout.

"Home, sweet home, kitties," Mayor Humdinger announced. "They'll never find us in here! Hurry inside, and don't forget the gold!"

They all ran into their hidden cave, but no one pulled the gold inside. Each of the kittens thought the other had brought it in!

Chase's drone led Ryder and the pups straight
to Humdinger's hideout.

"There's the gold!" Chase said. "Looks like
they left it behind!"

"Rocky, unhook that wagon," Ryder said.

"You got it!" exclaimed Rocky, heading for the
wagon full of gold.

Ryder had a plan to stop the sneaky kittens from following them. "Let it go, Rubble!" he shouted.

Rubble used his bulldozer to push a big boulder in front of the hideout's door. *WHUMP!* Mayor Humdinger and his Kit-tastrophe Crew were temporarily trapped!

"Nooo!" Mayor Humdinger cried as Ryder and the pups drove away with the wagon full of gold. "I deserve to be a statue!"

A few days later in Adventure Bay, Mayor Goodway unveiled a giant golden statue of Chickaletta. Ryder, Uncle Otis, and all the pups laughed when the little chicken perched on top.

"She loves it!" Mayor Goodway exclaimed. Everyone cheered for Chickaletta!

PUP-FU POWER!

Illustrated by Fabrizio Petrossi

In Farmer Yumi's barn, the PAW Patrol pups, Mayor Goodway, and Chickaletta practiced their Pup-Fu moves. Rubble flew through the air and kicked a board in half.

"Strong kick, Rubble!" Ryder cheered.

"Thanks, Ryder!" Rubble said.

"The pups have been working very hard," Farmer Yumi told Ryder. "They're ready to test for their yellow belts!"

"Students, begin," Farmer Yumi said to the PAW Patrol. The pups bowed to their teacher, then showed off their moves one by one.

Arf! Arf! Marshall barked as he spun on his tail, holding his paws out, ready for action!

Rocky used the grabber in his backpack to hold a staff. He twirled it, then planted it on the floor of the barn and vaulted over it.

"*Rrr-ruff! HA!*" Rocky cried as he struck a martial arts position.

Skye stood still for a moment, then flipped high into the air. As she turned a somersault, she kicked out in both directions. She landed on all fours.

"*Yip, yip! HA!*" Skye yelped as she kicked her paw straight out.

Zuma raised himself up on his back paws and held his
front paws out. He moved slowly and smoothly to the left.
Then he moved slowly and smoothly to the right. Zuma
was in complete control and ready for action!

On the floor, Rubble rolled to his left and kicked with his back leg. *"Hyyy-yah!"*

He rolled to his right and kicked with his other back leg. *"Hyyy-yah!"*

Finally, Rubble kicked with both legs. *"Hyyy-yah!"*

Chase announced, "And now I will—ah . . . ah . . . *CHOO!*"
Farmer Yumi looked concerned.

"Sorry," Chase explained, "I'm a little allergic to . . . kittens?"
He noticed a kitten standing next to him. "Ah-*CHOO!*" Chase
sneezed so hard, his headband flew off and landed on his nose.

Mayor Humdinger walked into the barn with the rest of his Kit-tastrophe Crew. "My kittens will get their yellow belts before the PAW Patrol," he bragged. "Because their Cat-Jitsu is better than Pup-Fu!"

"It's not about which art is superior," Mayor Goodway said. "The point is for all pups, kittens, mayors, and chickens to do their best!"

"Show them, kittens!" Mayor Humdinger said, clapping his hands. The Kit-tastrophe Crew lined up.

One by one, the kittens sprang into action. They jumped. They kicked. They twirled. They even balanced on a ball of yarn!

High in the rafters of the barn, one kitten set up a cable to slide down.

Marshall got there before the kitten. "I'll show you how a Pup-Fu master uses the zip line," he said.

He jumped up, grabbed the cord, and slid down it. "*Wheeee!*"

But when Marshall was halfway down, the kitten used its mechanical claw to tug on the zip line. The line shook, and Marshall went flying! "*Whoa!*"

THUMP! Marshall fell to the barn floor.

"Are you okay?" Rubble asked.

"Sure," Marshall answered. "A Pup-Fu master always knows exactly how to land when he accidentally falls."

"Next we will have the sparring part of our yellow belt test," Farmer Yumi said. "Begin!"

The pups and kittens began to spar. Marshall sprang over a kitten. Then he jumped back the other way, turning a somersault in midair.

The kitten launched a ball of yarn from her backpack, aiming it right at Marshall.

"*Whoa!*" he yelped as he fell to the floor. His legs were tangled in the yarn.

"Pup-Fu?" Mayor Humdinger snickered. "That looks more like pup *fail*!"

Farmer Yumi gave each pup a yellow belt. "Your extra-hard work would please the ancient masters," she said.

But there were no belts for the kittens.

"Mayor Humdinger," Farmer Yumi said, "until your kittens learn to control themselves and their tools, I'm afraid they cannot earn their yellow belts."

"Hooray for the PAW Patrol!" Ryder cheered. They were all good pups—and they were all very good sports!

PUP, PUP, AND AWAY!

Illustrated by Harry Moore

It was the day of the Annual Mayor's Balloon Race, and Mayor Goodway was nervous.

"Why did I ever agree to a balloon race?" she said, shaking her head. "I have to get over my fear of heights."

"Don't worry. I'll be in the balloon to help you," Ryder said. He turned to Chase and Rubble. "Ready to unroll the balloon?"

"We're ready!" Rubble said.

Rubble and Chase unrolled the balloon, pushing it with their noses.

"It sure is dusty!" Chase said.

Then he noticed something. "Uh-oh!" he said. "The balloon's got a . . . a . . . ah-*CHOO!*"

When he was done sneezing from the dust, Chase continued, "A rip! This balloon can't hold air!"

Mayor Goodway groaned. "Mayor Humdinger from Foggy Bottom will win again!"

"Don't worry," Ryder said. "We'll get this balloon ready for the race. No job is too big, no pup is too small!"

Ryder pulled out his PupPad and called the rest of the PAW Patrol.

The other members of the PAW Patrol jumped into their vehicles and raced to the town square with their sirens blaring.

Rocky inspected the tear in the balloon. "Hmm. I've got the perfect patch in my truck!"

"How does the gas tank look, Marshall?" Ryder asked.

"The big question is how does it smell?" Marshall replied. He sniffed. "I don't smell any gas leak."

Rocky glued a piece of Zuma's old surf kite over the hole.

"Good work!" Ryder exclaimed. "That patch is a perfect fit."

Ryder pulled a lever a little bit, and the balloon slowly filled with hot air. It rose above the basket that Mayor Goodway and Ryder would ride in.

The other balloons were gathering nearby. The race was about to begin!

"Time to win this race!" Mayor Goodway shouted. She pumped her fist and accidentally hit the heater lever, flipping it all the way open. The balloon started to fly away!

Marshall grabbed on to a rope dangling from the balloon and was lifted high into the air.

"Uh-oh!" he said. The rope slipped out of his mouth, and he fell!

Marshall landed right in Ryder's arms. "Nice catch, Ryder!" The pup gave Ryder a grateful lick. *SLUURP!*

The race had started, so there was no time to waste. Ryder called Skye on his PupPad.

"Mayor Goodway took off without me! I need you to fly me to her balloon in your copter!"

Skye slid down the Lookout's twisting slide into her
Pup House. She pressed a button, and it turned into her
helicopter.

"Let's take to the sky!" she shouted happily.

Skye zoomed into the air and flew to pick up Ryder.

Ryder snapped the harness he was wearing onto Skye's tow line. She lifted him up.

"I'll swing you over to the balloon," Skye told him. But she had to hurry because the balloon was headed straight for the lighthouse on Seal Island!

Ryder sailed through the air, reached out, and caught the basket!

Mayor Goodway helped Ryder climb into the balloon. He quickly gave it a burst of hot air, and it rose over the lighthouse.

"All right, Mayor Goodway," he said. "Are you ready to win this race?"

The mayor gave Ryder a thumbs-up. "I'm in it to win it!"

They raced after the other balloons.

As Ryder worked the controls, the balloon quickly
caught up with Mayor Humdinger, who was in the lead.
"The race is on!" Ryder yelled.
"I've never lost a race, and I'm not starting now!"
Mayor Humdinger shouted, shaking his fist angrily.

With a rush of hot air, Ryder and Mayor Goodway's balloon whooshed past Mayor Humdinger. "Don't worry!" Mayor Goodway called as she waved. "We'll wait for you—at the finish line!"

She spotted Jake's Mountain. "The finish line is on the other side!" she said.

"The winds are stronger up high," Ryder said. "We'll have a better chance of winning if we go up. What do you say?"

"Up, up, and away!" Mayor Goodway cheered.

Ryder guided the balloon higher and rode the rushing winds over Jake's Mountain—but so did Mayor Humdinger! His balloon zipped right past Ryder and Mayor Goodway!

Down on the ground, the PAW Patrol pups cheered as
the balloons came into view. Mayor Humdinger's balloon
swooped out of the sky first . . . but Mayor Goodway and
Ryder dropped ahead of him at the last second.

They snapped through the red finish line ribbon and
won the race!

Mayor Humdinger reluctantly handed the trophy over
to Mayor Goodway. "I believe this trophy belongs to you
this year."

Mayor Goodway gave the trophy to Ryder.
"This belongs to Ryder and the PAW Patrol," she said.
"Thanks, Mayor Goodway!" Ryder said with a big
smile. "Whenever you need a hand, just yelp for help!"

Chase's Space Case

Illustrated by MJ Illustrations

One starry night, Ryder, Skye, and Rocky were gazing up at the sky.

"A star is falling!" Skye said.

Ryder checked with his binoculars. "Hmm, that doesn't look like a star to me," he said. "It seems to be some kind of spaceship!"

"Cool!" Rocky and Skye said.

"And it's headed for Adventure Bay!" Ryder said.

CRASH! The spaceship slammed into Farmer Yumi's barn!

Strange glowing rings came out of the spaceship, and they formed a big green bubble around Farmer Yumi's cow, Bettina.

The bubble lifted Bettina into the air! *MOOOOO!*

Mayor Goodway was at a square dance in Farmer Yumi's barn. When she came out of the barn, she saw Bettina trapped in the floating bubble!

She called Ryder right away. "Can you help poor Bettina and find out what's going on here?"

"We're on it, Mayor Goodway," Ryder promised. "No job is too big, no pup is too small!"

Ryder called the other members of the PAW Patrol
and told them about Bettina's problem.
They jumped into their vehicles and raced to
Farmer Yumi's barn. The shining stars lit their way.
"PAW Patrol is on the roll!" Ryder shouted.

When they reached the barn, they saw Bettina still floating in the bubble.

"Weird," Chase said. "How does she stay up there?"

"I don't know," Ryder said. "But I think *this* might have something to do with it!" He pointed at the crashed spaceship.

With the suction cups from Chase's zip line, the pups pulled Bettina out of the green bubble.

"Chase, I need you to use your spy gear to find the pilot of that spaceship," Ryder said.

"Yes, sir, Ryder, sir!" Chase said. "Night-vision goggles!" Green goggles slid down from Chase's helmet to cover his eyes and help him see in the dark. He sniffed the ground, searching for the missing pilot.

Chase didn't find the pilot—he found Mayor Goodway and Chickaletta trapped in a floating bubble!

"How did you two get up there?" he cried.

"A little green space alien beamed us up!" Mayor Goodway explained.

Chase used the net in his backpack to pull the mayor and Chickaletta out of the green bubble. Then he continued his search for the little green space alien.

Chase found something. "A round green head!" He
looked closer. "Oops. It's just a melon."

He looked around and saw that he was in a field of
melons. He walked down one row. "Melon . . . melon . . .
space alien . . . melon . . . Wait—*space alien*?"

The little alien looked scared. *"Baw! Buh-bee! Buh-baw-baw-baw!"* he said.

"Sorry," said Chase, "but I don't understand what you're saying!"

The alien pointed at Chase, and yellow rings came out of his finger. A green bubble formed around the pup and lifted him up!

"Whoa!" Chase yelped.

The little green alien ran off, leaving Chase trapped in the floating bubble!

Chase tried to push his way out of the bubble, but he was stuck. "Help! Help! Anybody?" he called.

He got an idea. "If I can pull Bettina and the mayor free, I can pull myself out, too! Zip line!"

The zip line shot out of his backpack and attached itself to two trees. Chase slid down the line and out of the bubble!

The alien made his way to the Lookout—which looked like a spaceship to him!

Ryder and the pups found the alien trying to fly the Lookout. He wanted to go home to his mom.

Ryder pulled out his PupPad and made a call. "Rocky, how's it going with fixing that spaceship? Are you close?"

"Yes!" Rocky said. "Look out the window!"

Ryder, the pups, and the alien all ran to the window and saw Rocky flying the spaceship! He had fixed it with some old parts he'd found in his truck. A pink coat hanger made a fine antenna. A bicycle wheel worked as part of the landing gear.

"Don't lose it—reuse it!" Rocky said.

The alien hopped up and down happily. *"Bay-bay-bay-bay! Buh-bah-buh-bah!"*

Ryder kneeled and said to the alien, "Whenever you're in trouble, just yelp—or *beep-beep-beep*—for help! C'mon!" He led the way into the spaceship.

The happy little alien flew his new spaceship
with Rocky and Ryder in it. Then he beamed the
rest of the PAW Patrol aboard.

"We're flying in a spaceship!" Skye said. "Sweet!"

"Awesome!" the others agreed.

As they flew over Adventure Bay, they waved to
Mayor Goodway and Chickaletta.

"Coolest ride ever!" Ryder said.

The little green alien beamed the pups and
Ryder onto the field in front of the Lookout.
As the alien flew back to his home planet
and his family, Ryder and the PAW Patrol waved
goodbye to their new friend.

KING for a DAY!

Illustrated by MJ Illustrations

"Fear not, fair princess!" Marshall cried. "The Pups of the Round Table will save thee!"

The pups were practicing their play about knights. Chase was King Arthur, and the other pups were his brave knights.

"Our play will be *knight*-tastic!" Marshall declared.

In Adventure Bay's town square, Cap'n Turbot was
building the set for the play. The set looked like a castle!

"Castle construction is close to completion!" Cap'n
Turbot announced. "Just one last nail . . ."

But when he swung his hammer, he missed! Instead of
hitting the nail, he hit the castle wall, and . . .

. . . the set collapsed!

A big piece of the castle fell right on top of Cap'n Turbot.

"I'm stuck!" he cried. He reached for his phone and called the PAW Patrol for help.

"Don't worry, Cap'n Turbot," Ryder said. "No job is too big, no pup is too small!"

The PAW Patrol raced to the town square.

"How are you, Cap'n Turbot?" Marshall asked.

"Super! But stuck," he said. "And my arm smarts a smidge."

"We'll have you out in no time!" Ryder promised. "Rubble, use your claw hook to lift the wall."

"On the double!" Rubble said.

Rubble backed his truck up to the wall and
lifted it away from Cap'n Turbot. But there was
still another piece of scenery trapping him.
    Chase used the winch on his vehicle to pull the
doorway off Cap'n Turbot. He was free!
    "Thanks, PAW Patrol!" Cap'n Turbot said as
he stood and brushed himself off.

"Okay, Cap'n Turbot!" Marshall said. "I need to do a medical exam. X-ray machine!"

The machine popped out of Marshall's pack. He used it to scan Cap'n Turbot's bones.

"Hmm," Marshall said. "Looks like it's only a sprain. I'll wrap it up."

A bandage popped out of Marshall's pack. He wrapped the bandage around Cap'n Turbot's wrist.

Cap'n Turbot needed to rest his
arm, so it was up to the PAW Patrol to
finish building the castle for their play.
"Okay, my Pups of the Round
Table!" Chase commanded through his
megaphone. "Moveth!"
Skye used her helicopter and a
towing cable to fly a wall to the set. She
placed it in the middle of the stage.

Rocky popped a tool arm out of his pack. *ZZRRRZZZ!* He used the power screwdriver to spin screws through a hinge and into the wooden door. He tested the door to make sure it could easily open and close.

"This castle door is ready!" he announced.

Marshall held a paintbrush in his mouth and dipped it into a can of purple paint. He carefully spread the paint on the wall. Ryder worked on the other side of the doorway. Together, they finished painting the castle in a flash!

Soon the castle was ready! The pups felt so proud, they all howled and barked.

Except Chase. He didn't bark—he coughed!

Marshall took his temperature. "Uh-oh. You've got a fever! You need lots of rest and liquids."

But who would play King Arthur in the play?

Marshall! He knew all the lines! And the crown fit him.

It was time to start the entertainment, and
the last of the audience arrived just before the
play began. Cali the kitten was a princess stuck
high in a tower. The pup who pulled the bone
from the stone would become king and save
the princess.

"Behold! The bone!" Rubble said.

"Mmm," Rocky said, licking his lips.
"It looks-eth delicious!"

Marshall entered. "Fear not, fair princess!"

He jumped over the bone and took it in his teeth.
Then he struggled to pull it out of the stone.

WHOOOP! When the bone came free, it flew out
of Marshall's mouth and hit the tower! The tower
toppled over, and Cali fell!

The audience gasped!

Thankfully, Marshall caught Cali—and he remembered to say his line. "You are free, fair princess!"

The audience cheered. Marshall was doing an excellent job!

Lady Skye popped the wings out of her pack and flew over Marshall. "Heads up!" she said as she dropped a golden crown right onto his head.

It was a perfect fit!

"All hail King Arthur!" the pups cried, kneeling in front of Marshall.

The curtain closed. When it opened again, the pups took a bow. The audience cheered again!

"Great job, all of you!" Ryder said. "You're such good pups!"

The king had saved the day.

And Marshall had saved the play!

PIT CREW PUPS

Illustrated by MJ Illustrations

lex was a friend of the PAW Patrol. He called to his grandfather, "Hey, Grandpa! Check out what I made from old stuff from your restaurant. A Super Trike!"

"Very nice!" Grandpa said.

"Look," Alex said. "I made a brake out of a pizza paddle!"

"And you used lots of duct tape!" Grandpa said.

"Just like you taught me," Alex said.

"Watch this, Grandpa!" Alex said. "I'm going to go super fast on my Super Trike!"

First he tightened his helmet. Then he grabbed the handlebars, ran as fast as he could, jumped in, and pedaled hard.

"Whoo-hoo!" he cried as he raced down the sidewalk.

But the Super Trike hit a little bump and flew into the air.
WHUMP! When the bike landed, it fell apart.

"My Super Trike!" Alex wailed.

Parts flew everywhere. Some even rolled into the street.

"Now I have to put it all back together again," Alex said sadly.

"I know who can help you!" Grandpa said.

Grandpa called Ryder.

"Hello?" Ryder said. "Ryder here."

"Hi, Ryder," Grandpa said. "I have a bit of an emergency."

He explained what happened to Alex's bike. "I know you're pretty handy with gadgets and vehicles."

"Tell him we're on our way!" Ryder said. "No job is too big, no pup is too small!"

Ryder called the PAW Patrol. They jumped into
their vehicles and zoomed across the bridge to town.
VROOOOM!
Ryder led the way on his four-wheeler.
Chase drove his customized squad car.
Rocky followed in his repair truck.
And Skye flew overhead in her helicopter!

"Let's secure the work zone," Chase said. In the street, he put orange cones around the scattered parts of Alex's Super Trike.

Next he spoke to the drivers through his megaphone. "Please find an alternate route. PAW Patrol at work!"

The cars turned around and drove down a different street.

Ryder and Alex picked up the parts.

"Can you fix it?" Alex asked.

"Sure we can!" Ryder said.

Back at the Lookout, Ryder, Rocky, and Chase put the Super Trike back together. They also added some new parts. And instead of duct tape, they used screws and rivets to fasten the parts together.

"These will hold better," Rocky said.

"But my grandpa fixes *everything* with duct tape," Alex said.

"I think it's done!" Ryder announced.

"Awesome!" Alex shouted. "Now my Super Trike can go super fast! C'mon, Ryder! Let's race!"

"First we need to test it, and then you need to get used to it," Ryder said. "Try riding it slowly."

But Alex didn't want to go slowly. He jumped on his Super Trike and took off, pedaling as hard as he could.

"Alex, wait!" Ryder called. "You're going too fast!"

Alex zoomed down a hill. "Wow, this is fast!"

But it was *too* fast. Alex took his feet off the pedals.

Ryder rode up behind him. "Slow down! Use the brakes!"

"I can't get my feet back on the pedals!" Alex cried.
"They're turning too fast!"

Ryder looked ahead and saw that Alex was racing right
toward a busy street!

"Chase!" Ryder yelled. "Secure the traffic!"

"Chase is on the case!" he called. He took a shortcut down a hill with his lights flashing and his siren blaring. He pulled into traffic.

"Please stop!" he said to the drivers. "PAW Patrol emergency in progress!" All the cars stopped.

Just then, Alex and Ryder zipped by onto the bridge.

Ryder called Skye. "I need you and your copter at the bridge!"

"Let's take to the sky!" she said.

Skye flew straight to the bridge. Then she lowered a hook
to catch the back of Alex's trike to slow him down.

She missed it twice, but on her third try, she did it! "Got
him!" she said.

The trike stopped. Alex got off and waved up to Skye. "Yay, Skye! Great flying!"

"That *was* some pretty good flying," Ryder agreed.

"Aw," Skye said modestly. "It was no biggie."

"Are you all right, Alex?" Ryder asked.

"I'm okay," he said. "I just couldn't stop it. My Super Trike is *too* super!"

The pups joined Ryder and Alex on the bridge.
"I'm sorry, Ryder," Alex said. "This is all my fault.
If I had slowed down like you said, this wouldn't
have happened."

"That's okay, Alex," Ryder said. "But whenever
you try something new, you have to start out easy."

Alex nodded and smiled. "I know. I just wanted
to be like you, Ryder!"

"You were such good pups today, how about we head to the lemonade stand?" Ryder suggested.

"Yeah!" Alex cheered, ringing the bell on his Super Trike. "Let's race on over!"

Skye cleared her throat, and Chase shook his head.

"I mean *roll* on over," Alex said.

They all got into their vehicles and rode to the lemonade stand safely.

"Good work, Alex!" Ryder said. "You've earned the PAW Patrol Safe Driving Cup." He handed Alex a trophy.

"Wowie!" Alex said. "Thanks, Ryder!"

"You've also won a spoon," Ryder added.

Alex looked confused. "A spoon? Why?"

Ryder took the top off the trophy. It was full of ice cream! "'Cause it's an *ice cream* cup!"

"Yay!" Alex cheered.

RUBBLE'S BIG WISH

Illustrated by Harry Moore

ocky and Rubble were helping Farmer Al sort through some old stuff in his barn. Rubble dug into a pile of toys.

"Hey, a jack-in-the-box!" he said. "I'm going to clean it up and play with it!" He yawned. "Right after I take a little nap."

Rubble curled up next to the toy, and soon he was asleep. He began to dream. . . .

The jack-in-the-box started to jump around. Rubble turned the box's handle, and music began to play. And then . . . a genie popped out of the box! Rubble and Rocky gasped.

"Pleased to meet you!" the genie said. "I'm Jeremy the Genie. Since you let me out of that box, you get three wishes! What would you like?"

"Hmm," Rubble said, thinking. "What do I really want? I know! A bone that'll last forever!"

Jeremy led Rubble and Rocky outside, where there was plenty of room.

"Grant this wish to a pup so clever—one big bone that'll last forever!" the genie chanted.

The genie used his magic to make a giant bone appear in the sky!

"Wow! My wishbone!" Rubble said.

The bone hovered in the air for a moment, but then it fell onto the barn. *CRASH!* It was stuck in a big hole in the roof!

"I just graduated from Genie School," Jeremy admitted, "so I'm new at this."

Farmer Al ran out of his barn and stared at the giant bone.

"Don't worry, Farmer Al," Rubble said. "We'll get Ryder!"

Rubble and Rocky ran to the Lookout. They told Ryder about the genie, and the bone that broke the roof of Farmer Al's barn.

"We'll take care of it," Ryder promised. "No wish is too big, no pup is too small!"

Ryder called the other members of the PAW Patrol and came up with a plan. They all hurried back to the barn.

"Rubble," Ryder said, "use your crane to lift the bone off the roof."

"Rubble on the double!" the pup exclaimed.

Rubble lowered his claw to grab the giant bone. Then he raised it out of the hole in the roof.

"Good job, Rubble!" Ryder shouted.

"Okay, Skye," Ryder called. "You can fly Rocky and his supplies up there now."

"You got it, Ryder!" Skye answered.

She flew her helicopter to the roof, carrying Rocky on a platform. Rocky had some old cupboard doors and shingles with him to repair the hole.

"Green means go!" Rocky howled.

"Hammer!" Rocky said. His backpack opened, and a hammer popped out. He started hammering the old cupboard doors over the hole in the roof.

"Wow!" Jeremy said. "I can help with that!"

Using his genie magic, Jeremy floated the shingles into place. Rocky nailed them down in record time!

The roof was fixed!

"Good as new!" Farmer Al said. "Thank you, PAW Patrol!"

Rubble set the giant bone on the ground. He and the other pups ran over to it. Rubble gave it a lick.

"Yummy!" he said. "It's so big, it'll last forever! I'm happy to share it with my friends!"

Jeremy told Rubble he still had two wishes left.

As Rubble thought, he wandered around, not watching where he was going. *SPLOOSH!* He slipped and fell into a mud puddle!

"Yuck!" Rubble said. "Now I know what I want. I wish for the super-bubbliest bubble bath ever!"

"*This pup likes it in the tub-ly—make it warm and super bubbly!*" Jeremy chanted.

Rubble's bubble bath was so bubbly, one giant
bubble formed around the tub and lifted it into the air!
"I think I'm in bubble trouble!" Rubble whimpered.
But as he floated along in his bathtub, Rubble started
to enjoy himself.
"This is fun!" he said.

Rubble saw a row of pine trees up ahead.

"Pine trees?" he said. "Oh, no! One thing about pines—they sure are prickly!"

POP! The prickly pines popped Rubble's big bubble! He fell through the tree . . . and landed on a limb hanging over a river!

Rubble called Ryder for help.

"We're on our way!" Ryder said.

Ryder put on a harness, and Skye lowered him from her helicopter to the pine tree.

"A little lower, Skye!" Ryder called. "Hang tight, Rubble!"

CRACK! Just as the tree branch broke and the tub began to fall, Ryder scooped up Rubble!

"Gotcha!" he said.

"Thanks, Ryder!" said Rubble, giving him a big lick.

"What's your last wish, Rubble?" Jeremy asked.

"I wish I could do something nice for all my friends," Rubble answered.

"Good pups deserve lots of good eats—reward these pups with tons of treats!" the genie chanted.

KA-BOOM! There was a loud clap of thunder, and then it started to rain puppy treats!

"Yay!" the pups cheered. . . .

In the barn, Ryder gently shook Rubble awake.
"Time to go home. Farmer Al said you were a big help."
"I'll say," said Farmer Al. "You good pups deserve
some good treats!"
He tossed treats to Rubble and Rocky. But Rubble
said, "No, thanks. I ate a bunch from the sky."
Ryder looked confused. "Are you all right?"
"Barns give me weird dreams," Rubble said, giggling.